www.mascotbooks.com

A House Divided

©2020 Erin Lough and Mave Lough Duke. All Rights Reserved. No part of this publication may be reproduced, stored in a retrieval system or transmitted in any form by any means electronic, mechanical, or photocopying, recording or otherwise without the permission of the author.

All Auburn University indicia are protected trademarks or registered trademarks of Auburn University and are used under license.

All University of Alabama indicia are protected trademarks or registered trademarks of The University of Alabama and are used under license.

Photo Credit to Corey Edwards, Aubie Program

For more information, please contact:
Mascot Books
620 Herndon Parkway #320
Herndon, VA 20170
info@mascotbooks.com

CPSIA Code: PRT0919A
ISBN-13: 978-1-68401-947-2

Printed in the United States

A HOUSE DIVIDED

This book is dedicated, in equal shares, to the fans
of Alabama and Auburn, to share and share alike, in all of our
Iron Bowl victories, as we represent the great state of Alabama.
Thank you to both Universities for making this book happen.

– Erin & Mave

It was Saturday morning and the big game was here;
they had waited for the IRON BOWL the *entire* year!
Emma dressed in orange and Russell wore crimson red.
They argued about whose team would come out ahead!

The parents watched as they played in the yard.
The kids ran FAST and threw the football HARD!

The Auburn vs. Alabama rivalry was always *the best;* but this game put the teams *and* their fans to the test.

All of a sudden, there was *chaos* outside!
Aubie shouted, "WAR EAGLE!"
and Big Al yelled, "ROLL TIDE!"

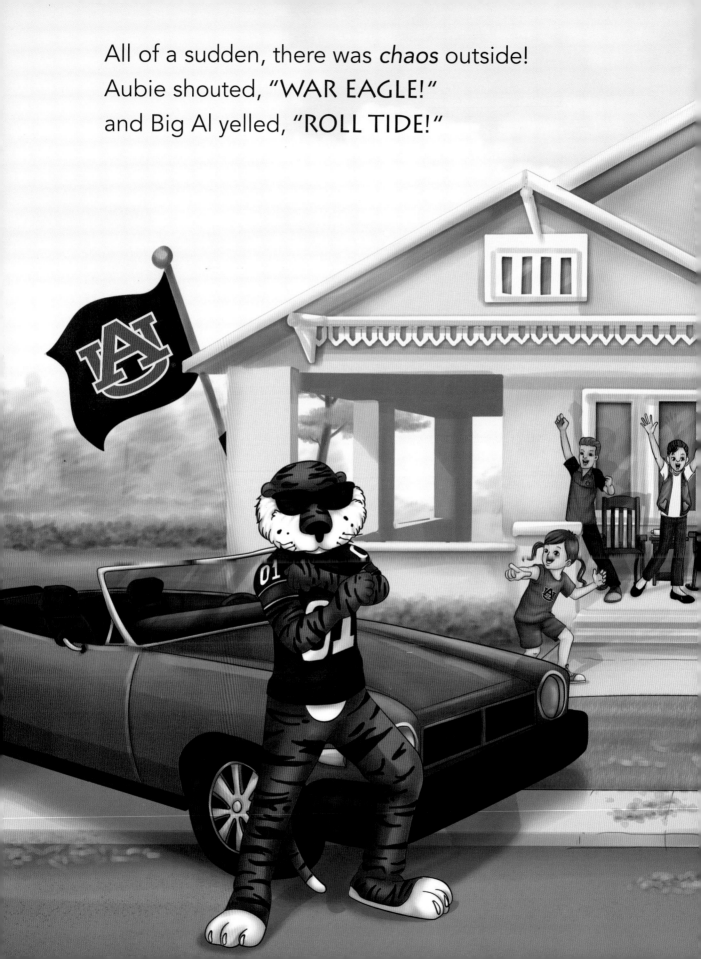

It was a dream come true!
The children couldn't believe their eyes!
These mascots were two of the COOLEST guys!

They went into the house and had a standoff in the room!
Each team stood on their side (*no one was crossing soon*).

The mascots had come over to their house to play,
and cheer for their team on IRON BOWL game day!

The game was on! Who would be the *first* to score?
It was the moment they had all been waiting for!
The football was kicked, and excitement filled the air!
But you could feel tension *(division also lived there)*.

Big Al shouted,
"LET THE GAMES BEGIN!
My team is #1, and we
will *definitely* win!"

Aubie shook his head
and stomped his feet.
"We are FAMILY!
Our spirit can't be beat!"

Big Al raised his trunk
and sounded it loudly.
He beat his chest and
stampeded proudly.

Aubie shook his head
and rolled his eyes.
"Our team is AU–SOME
and *full of surprises!*"

Aubie made a costume
with pom-poms to cheer.

Big Al grabbed a football,
"Stand back and *stay clear!*"

They laughed at the mascots while they joked;
Aubie held up his foam finger and Big Al choked!
Emma and Russell hoped this day would never end.
The mascots were their new silly friends!

During halftime, they went out to enjoy the weather, and decided the competition could be *even better!*

The family joined the mascots to play tug-of-war; everyone pulled harder than they *ever had before!*

The mascots fell to the ground!
They both felt sore. (*This game
didn't seem so much fun anymore.*)

They had used their muscles to pull
with *all* of their might! (*This rivalry had
quickly turned into more of a fight!*)

The children's eyes were filled with tears.
"You two have been fighting for *so many years!*"

"We think it's time to shake hands
with one another. After all, what would
life be like WITHOUT *the other*?!"

The mascots were confused and thought, "WHAT IF they're RIGHT?! This house has been divided long enough! It's time to UNITE!"

"We have so much passion for *both* of our teams;
it's okay to let the other have his *own* dreams!"

"And as for the team that doesn't win,
there's no need to be ugly and rub it in!
Both of our teams represent the same state,
and having them *both* makes Alabama GREAT!"

The children were happy and their
smiles grew wide; it finally happened!
They were sitting on the same side!

That year was different, as they sat and shared a meal. They were thankful for each other (and it was really **NO BIG DEAL!**)

"WE MAY NOT HAVE IT ALL TOGETHER, BUT TOGETHER WE HAVE IT ALL."

–Unknown